Her Seven Brothers

Also by Paul Goble

Custer's Last Battle
The Fetterman Fight
Lone Bull's Horse Raid
The Friendly Wolf
The Girl Who Loved Wild Horses
The Gift of the Sacred Dog
Star Boy
Buffalo Woman
The Great Race
Death of the Iron Horse
Iktomi and the Boulder
Beyond the Ridge
Iktomi and the Berries
Dream Wolf
Iktomi and the Ducks
I Sing for the Animals
Iktomi and the Buffalo Skull
Crow Chief
Love Flute
The Lost Children

Aladdin Paperbacks

Her Seven Brothers

Story and illustrations by

Paul Goble

For Robert

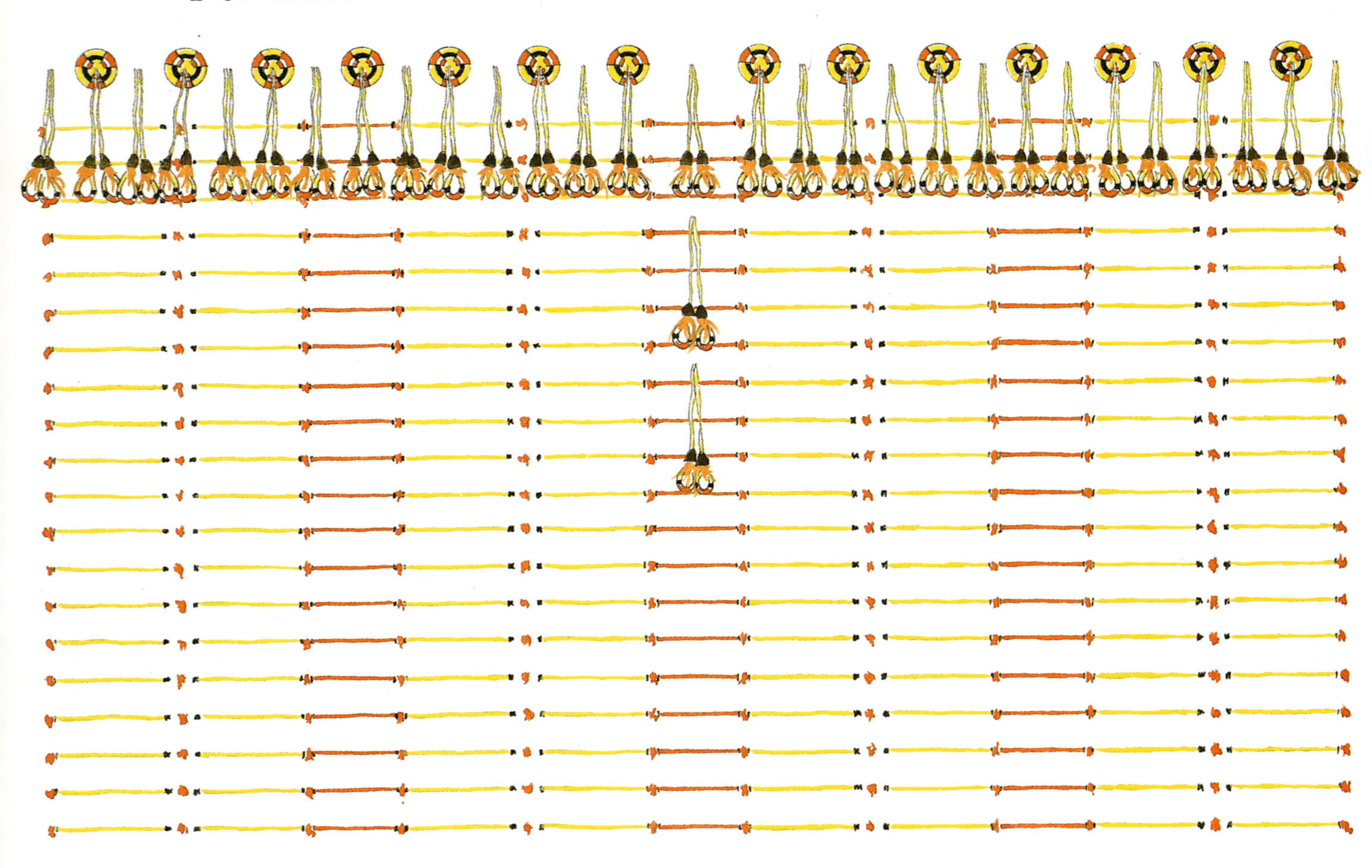

Aladdin Paperbacks. An imprint of Simon & Schuster Children's Publishing Division. 1230 Avenue of the Americas, New York, NY 10020. First Aladdin Paperbacks edition 1993. Also available in a hardcover edition from Simon & Schuster Books for Young Readers. Manufactured in China. 1011 SCP
20 19 18 17

Library of Congress Cataloging-in-Publication Data. Goble, Paul. Her seven brothers / story and illustrations by Paul Goble. p. cm. Summary: Retells the Cheyenne legend in which a girl and her seven chosen brothers become the Big Dipper. ISBN 0-689-71730-X 1. Cheyenne Indians—Legends. 2. Ursa Major—Folklore—Juvenile literature. [1. Cheyenne Indians—Legends. 2. Indians of North America—Great Plains—Legends. 3. Stars—Folklore.] I. Title. E99.C53G64 1993
398.2'08997—dc20 [E] 92-40562
(ISBN-13: 978-0-689-71730-7)

A NOTE FROM THE AUTHOR

The designs of the shirts and dresses and various other articles in this book are based on Cheyenne designs. These articles can be seen in many museums in both the United States and Europe. The designs of the painted tipis are taken from models that were made by Cheyennes about 1900 for the Field Museum of Natural History in Chicago.

The birds and animals, the flowers and butterflies share the earth with us, and so they are included in the pictures. Sometimes two of each are drawn; they, like us, enjoy each other's company. In other places many are drawn, reminding us of the Creator's generosity. They all live on the Great Plains, where this story takes place.

The illustrations are drawn with pen and India ink. When a drawing is finished, it looks much like a page from a child's painting book. The drawings are then filled in with watercolor, which is often applied rather thickly. Thin white lines are left, to try and achieve the brightness of Indian bead and quillwork, and to capture something of the bright colors that one sees in the clear air of the Great Plains.

REFERENCES for this Cheyenne story: Richard Erdoes and Alfonso Ortiz, *American Indian Myths and Legends*, Pantheon Books, New York, 1984; George Bird Grinnell, *By Cheyenne Campfires*, Yale University Press, New Haven, 1926; John Stands in Timber and Margot Liberty, *Cheyenne Memories*, Yale University Press, New Haven, 1967; A. L. Kroeber, "Cheyenne Tales," *The Journal of American Folk-lore*, Vol. XIII, No. 1, 1900; Carrie A. Lyford, *Quill and Beadwork of the Western Sioux*, Washington, DC, 1940; Alice Marriott, *The Trade Guild of the Southern Cheyenne Women*, Oklahoma Anthropological Society, 1937.

STORIES were told after dark when the mind's eye sees most clearly. Winter evenings were best, when the children were lying under their buffalo robes and the fire was glowing at the center of the tipi. After the sounds in the camp had grown quiet and the deer had come out to graze, the storyteller would smooth the earth in front of him; rubbing his hands together, he would pass them over his head and body. He was remembering that the Creator had made people out of the earth, and would be witness to the truth of the story he was going to tell.

DO you know what the birds and animals say?

In the old days there were more people who understood them. The Creator did not intend them to speak in our way; theirs is the language of the spirits. Yes, birds and animals, butterflies and beetles, stones and trees still speak to us; but we have to learn how to listen.

In those distant times there was a girl who lived with her parents. She did not have any brothers or sisters, but she was never alone because she could speak with the birds and animals. She understood the spirits of all things.

When the girl was quite young her mother taught her how to embroider with dyed porcupine quills onto deer and buffalo skin robes and clothes. She worked hard. In time she became very good at it. Her parents were proud when she gave away something she had made. People marveled at her skill and beautiful designs. They believed that Porcupine, who climbs trees closest to Sun himself, had spoken to the girl and given her mysterious help to do such wonderful work. While the girl worked, she kept good thoughts in her mind; she knew that she could not make anything beautiful without help from the spirits.

One day she started to sew clothes for a man: a shirt and a pair of moccasins. She decorated them with porcupine quills in brightly colored patterns. Every design had a meaning for her.

When the shirt and moccasins were finished, she did not give them to anyone; she put them away and started on another set. Her parents wondered why she did this when she had neither brothers nor young men who were courting her. When a second set was finished and she was starting another, her mother asked her for whom she was making the clothes.

Her daughter replied: "There are seven brothers who live by themselves far in the north country where the cold wind comes from. I have seen them in my mind when I close my eyes. I am making the clothes for them. They have no sister. I will look for the trail that leads to their tipi. I will ask them to be my brothers."

At first her mother thought it was just a young girl's imagining, but every day her daughter brought out her work. The months passed, and she made six shirts and pairs of moccasins. And then she started with special care on a seventh set, smaller than the others, to fit a very small boy. Her mother was puzzled, and yet she sensed that her daughter had seen something wonderful. Even the wise men did not know, but they believed that the unseen powers had spoken to the girl.

Her mother said: "I will go with you. When the snow melts we will pack your gifts onto the dogs. I will help you guide them until you find the trail."

The geese brought back the springtime, and they set out for the north country. The way was green and beautiful with flowers; and loud with frogs and red-winged blackbirds calling by every pond. Two faithful dogs carried the bags of clothes. The girl had the little boy's clothes in a separate bundle on her back.

When the girl found the trail, she said to her mother: "This is where I will go on alone. Mother, do not be sad! You will be proud! Soon you will see me again with my brothers; everyone will know and love us!"

But her mother did cry. She called to the sun: "O Sun, look after my child!" She watched her daughter, leading a dog at either hand, walk away and fade slowly into the immensity of the blue distance.

The girl walked on for many days into the land of pine trees until she came at last to a tipi pitched close to a lake. It was painted yellow and had stars all over it. The door was partly open; she thought she could see bright eyes peering at her from inside.

She unpacked the bags from the dogs. After they had taken a drink at the lake, she thanked them. "Now go straight back home," she told them. "Keep to the trail, and do not chase rabbits."

A little boy ran out of the tipi and called to her: "I am glad you have come! I have been waiting for you! You have come looking for brothers. I have six older brothers. They are away hunting buffalo, but they will be back this evening. They will be surprised to see you; they do not have my power of knowing and seeing. I am glad to call you 'Sister.' "

The girl opened the bundle of clothes she had made for him. "Younger Brother," she said, "this is my gift to you."

The boy had never seen anything so beautiful; his clothes had always been plain, and often old. He put on his new shirt and moccasins and scampered down to the lake to take a look at himself in the water. The girl untied the other bags, and placed a shirt and pair of moccasins on each of the six beds around the tipi.

When the little boy heard his brothers returning, he ran out of the tipi to meet them. "Wherever did you get those fine clothes?" they asked.

The boy replied: "A girl made them for me. She came looking for brothers, and now I call her 'Sister.' She has made wonderful shirts for all of you. Come and see!"

The brothers were very proud of their sister and looked after her well. While they were out hunting, she stayed in the tipi with the little boy. He would take his bow and arrows to protect her if she went out for water or to gather firewood. She liked to have good meals ready for the hunters when they returned home.

They all lived happily together until a day when a little buffalo calf came to the tipi. He scratched at the door with his hoof. The boy went outside and asked: "What do you want, Buffalo Calf?"

"I have been sent by the chief of the Buffalo Nation," the calf said. "He wants your sister. Tell her to follow me."

"He cannot have her," the boy answered. "My sister is happy here. We are proud of her."

The calf ran away, but in a little while a yearling bull galloped up to the tipi and bellowed: "I have been sent by the chief of the Buffalo Nation. He insists on having your sister. Tell her to come."

"No! He will never have her," the boy answered. "Go away!"

It was not long before an old bull with sharp curved horns charged up and thundered: "The chief of the Buffalo Nation demands your sister *now*! She must come *at once*, or he will come with the whole Buffalo Nation and get her, and you will all be killed." He shook his mane and whipped his back with his tail in rage.

"No!" the boy shouted. "He will never have her. Look! There are my big brothers coming back. *Hurry*, or they will surely kill you!"

When the brothers heard what had happened they were afraid. Even then they sensed an uncertain rumble, like shaking deep down inside the earth. Beyond the horizon dark dust clouds were rolling out across the sky toward them. The Buffalo People were stampeding in the awful darkness beneath.

"Run!" shouted one of the brothers.

"Wait!" the little boy called out, and he ran into the tipi for his bow and arrows. He shot an arrow straight up into the air and a pine tree appeared, growing upward with the arrow's flight.

The girl quickly lifted her little brother onto the lowest branch and climbed up after him. All the brothers clambered after, just as the Chief of the Buffalo struck the tree a terrible blow, splintering it with his horns. He hooked at the trunk again and again and it was split into slivers. Dark masses of angry buffalo crowded around the tree, pawing the ground and bellowing. The tree quivered and started to topple.

"Hurry! You have power. Save us!" the brothers called to the little boy. He shot an arrow and the tree grew taller.

He shot another far into the sky and the tree grew straight upward, higher and higher, and they were carried far away up among the stars.

And there they all jumped down from the branches onto the boundless star-prairies of the world above.

The girl and her seven brothers are still there. They are the Seven Stars in the northern sky, which we call the Big Dipper. But look carefully and you will see that there are really eight stars in the Big Dipper; close to one of them there is a tiny star; it is the little boy walking with his sister. She is never lonely now. They are forever turning around the Star Which Always Stands Still, the North Star. It is good to know that they once lived here on earth.

Listen to the stars! We are never alone at night.